If You Ever
Meet a Skeleton

For Mom, because you always cheer the loudest. — R. E.

For Michael, Sarah, Marie, and Alex. — K. D.

Text copyright © 2021 Rebecca Evans
Illustrations copyright © 2021 Katrin Dreiling

First published in 2021 by Page Street Kids
an imprint of
Page Street Publishing Co.
27 Congress Street, Suite 105
Salem, MA 01970
www.pagestreetpublishing.com

Distributed by Macmillan, sales in Canada by The Canadian Manda Group

21 22 23 24 25 CCO 5 4 3 2 1
ISBN-13: 978-1-64567-215-9. ISBN-10: 1-64567-215-8.

CIP data for this book is available from the Library of Congress.

This book was typeset in Paperboy. The illustrations were done using mixed media and compiled digitally.
Cover and book design by Melia Parsloe for Page Street Kids.
Printed and bound in Shenzhen, Guangdong, China

Page Street Publishing uses only materials from suppliers who are committed to
responsible and sustainable forest management.

Page Street Publishing protects our planet by donating to nonprofits like The Trustees,
which focuses on local land conservation.

If You Ever
Meet a Skeleton

Rebecca Evans   illustrated by Katrin Dreiling

PAGE
STREET
KiDS

One night a year on Halloween,
when magic's all around,

waking from their slumber . . .
skeletons climb out of the ground!

Skeletons might seem spooky—
white bones without the skin,
no eyes, no ears, no lips,
just one big toothy grin.

But if you meet a skeleton
some dark and gloomy night,
you shouldn't be afraid.
Old bones can't hurt you, right?

Skeletons have no muscle—
they'll never win a race.
Their legs flop 'round like jelly,
and they fall down on their face.

Skeletons have no brain—
it's slowly turned to goo.
They can't play hide-and-seek,
'cause they can't count to two.

Skeletons have no skin—
they often feel quite bare.
That's why they're always cold . . .
they're naked everywhere!

Skeletons have no nose—
they cannot smell your boots.
Not even when they stink
like Taco Tuesday toots.

Skeletons have no guts,
so they aren't brave like you.

They're scared of nighttime shadows
and owls that say "whoooo."

Skeletons have no friends.
They'd like to find a few:
some kids with stinky feet
and little brothers, too.

Skeletons *do* have teeth
but don't eat kids for food
because they're hard to chew;
plus, biting friends is rude.

Skeletons like to smile
at stories in the dark
about your ninja skills,
or when you caught a shark.

Skeletons are just bones.
They rattle, groan, and creak.

But they're the very best
at making mothers . . .

Skeletons make great friends—
they'll trick-or-treat with you
then share their chocolate bar,
just like best buddies do.